SLIME TIME FUN

Written by Franklin Smith
& Ali Crocker

Illustrated by Mark Marderosian

Inspired by Paul Lazowski

Educational Advisory Consultants

Ali Crocker, M.Ed   Michelle Gardner, MD

Michael Wojciechowski, President & CEO
Kids Klub Child Development Centers

Catherine Constantin-Reid
Founder of Grace Montessori School, Allentown

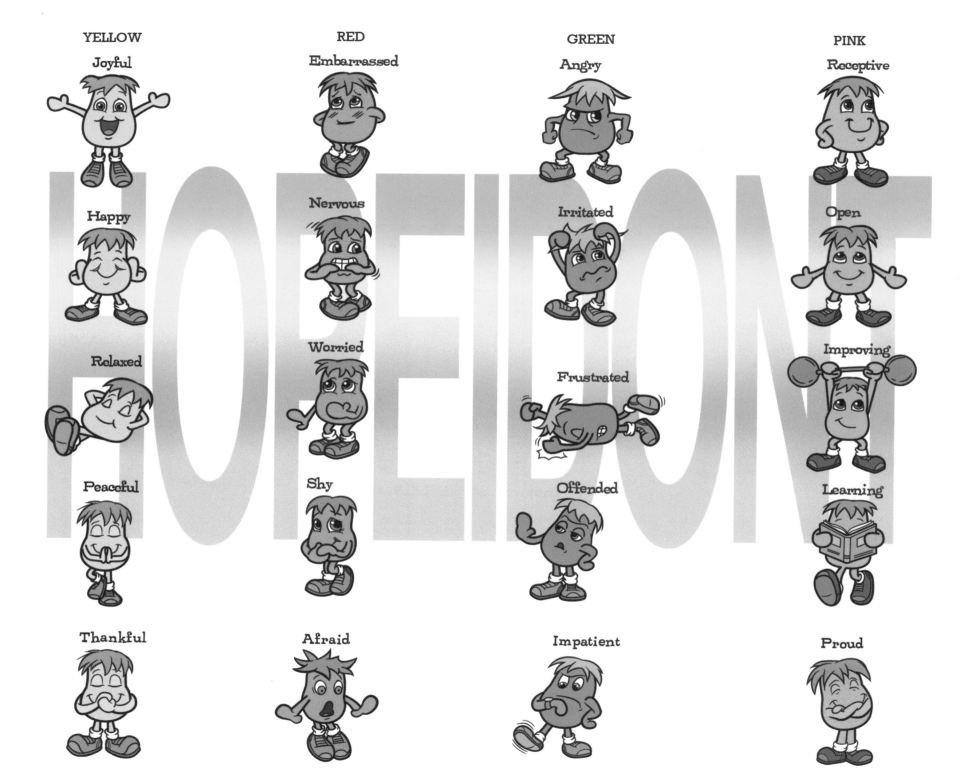

YELLOW

Joyful

Happy

Relaxed

Peaceful

Thankful

RED

Embarrassed

Nervous

Worried

Shy

Afraid

GREEN

Angry

Irritated

Frustrated

Offended

Impatient

PINK

Receptive

Open

Improving

Learning

Proud

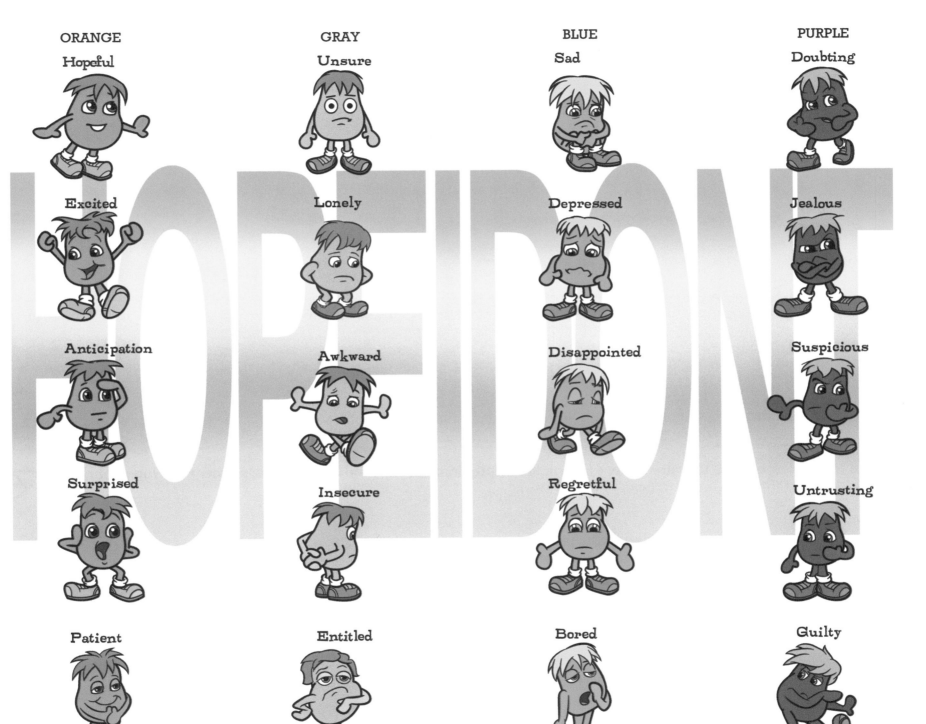

**Learning at home, with friends, or at school with your favorite teacher
helps kids understand how a Hopeidont is a unique creature.**

Nobody knows your child better than you, so we created fun lessons for you to do. You may want to read them while they follow along, or let them show you how learning to read makes them strong. We want this to be fun for you both, while your relationship sees new growth.

What is a Hopeidont?

There are forty Hopeidonts that are always whispering in your child's ears, some make them laugh, learn or smile; some make them sad or full of fear. Understanding these emotions can be confusing so guess what they need? Someone who can model good behavior and help plant a learning seed. That someone always shows them what to do, and you guessed it right, that someone is you.

There are EIGHT colors that Hopeidonts change into: yellow, red, green, pink, orange, gray, blue, purple.

Yellow
When the Hopeidont is happy, thankful, joyful, relaxed, or at peace, you will see their smile and positive attitude greatly increase.

Red
When the Hopeidont is turning to different shades of red, they are nervous, afraid, shy, worried, or embarrassed at what was said.

Green
Getting angry, irritated, impatient, frustrated, or offended is when the green Hopeidont says the peace has now ended.

Pink
When a Hopeidont is pink, they are ready to learn, are improving, proud, open or receptive, so the pink Hopeidonts are very special, and are known to be very perceptive.

Orange
When a Hopeidont is orange, it is full of anticipation, patient, surprised, hopeful, or excited, and it's very common that an orange Hopeidont is present when a wrong has been righted.

Gray
If you've ever felt awkward, unsure, lonely, entitled, or insecure, you may have a gray Hopeidont whispering in your ear.

Blue
Being regretful, disappointed, bored, depressed, or sad means a Hopeidont is blue, and that always feels bad.

Purple
When a Hopeidont is purple, it's full of doubt, guilty, jealous, suspicious, and untrusting; that's the time when a kid needs a real serious attitude adjusting.

Learning can be hard so we tried to make it fun, and included all kinds of teaching under the sun.
It's true we don't all learn the same, so let's review the learning style names.

Verbal
When you like to use words both in speech and in writing, learning can be very fun and sometimes exciting. Using words help some kids understand what they learn, so we are introducing words that will give everyone a turn. A turn to try a new word, and it may be more than a few. If they get confused you will be there to give them a clue.

Visual
When we use images, pictures and diagrams to get smarter, working with a crayon and pictures is a very helpful starter. Coloring with purpose helps get knowledge, and more knowledge is a clear path to college.

Musical/Auditory
When we use rhythm, sounds and rhymes, some people have the best learning times. Lets not forget to have fun when we grow. Rhythms and rhymes help us learn when we are high or low.

Physical/Kinesthetic
Using our hands, body and sense of touch, helps when frustration becomes a crutch. Getting your child involved with their hands helps them learn fast, and you are right there to help when questions are asked.

Logical/Mathmatical
Learning is easier for some when they use logic, systems, or reason, so we want to help your child think, which to them can be very pleasing. Good character is founded in logic and common sense, and this helps so that learning for your child is not so tense.

Social
When kids get to explain what's in their brain, understanding learning is not such a pain. Explaining to you what they know, might be just what they need to grow.

Solitary
Is it possible that some like to learn alone? Then imagine how fast they will learn when they have some time on their own. You get a break, so sit back and admire the small spark of learning that's becoming a fire.

Combination
Yes, it's true we all learn differently, especially when it's something new, but using a few of these styles won't compare to what they learn from you.

Dedicated to Grandparents:

I can't imagine how my life would be
without family and friends that believe in me.
The list is long of those that have believed,
who've helped me to finish this dream I've achieved.
I will thank you and thank you until my days are gone
For believing when I was right and correcting when I was wrong.

Learning to say thank you, that's not so hard,
Saying it from my heart is the important part.
If I have not said thank you, then please let me say it now.
I'll say it again and again, as long as my breath will allow.

But if you are a grandparent who has made a child smile,
I dedicate this to you, for giving an inch and loving a mile.

- Franklin Smith

Library of Congress Control Number: 2022914739

ISBN: 978-1-955043-99-1 HC
ISBN: 978-1-955043-98-4 PB

Printed in Canada

HOPEiDONT BOOKS
Order books exclusively at
www.hopeidont.com
Visit us on Facebook!

SLIME TIME FUN

What color is your Hopeidont today?

I'm feeling angry!

I don't like how this feels.

Maybe there's a different way.

I'm feeling better already.

Happy feels much better!

Have you ever seen a mountain with tall, tall trees?
Where rivers run deep, and in winter they freeze?
A mountain that will give you pretty little flowers
And giant mud puddles when the mountain gets showers?

Now imagine the fun that you could have if you tried
To run up the mountain and slide down the other side.
What if you could climb to the top of the trees?
You just might imagine what a bigfoot sees.

The mountain has two bigfoots that play all day long.
One is short and smart, the other tall and strong.
They live in different homes, but they are **best** friends.
And the one thing they hope for is that the fun never ends.

They have squatchbikes and squatchboards to ride down the road.
They eat squatchbars and puddle brew. They scarf the whole load.
There was no end to the fun these bigfoots knew.
They even used slime to make green stew.

Now, today the rain was really making a mess.
Budger said, "Let's play inside." Buz finally said, "Yes."
They got out their pots and made squatchhog stew.
And added every ingredient into the boiling brew.

Once the two were ready to sit down and eat,
They called in Grandmasquatch, and she took a seat.
The table was covered from the slime they brought in—
It got on Buz's face, his head and his chin.

The rain had stopped, and the sun was now shining.
Instead of cleaning up, Buz started his whining.
He didn't want to do his part and clean up the slime.
All he wanted to do was have a good bigfoot time.

Buz was so frustrated, while Budger's patience grew.
Buz wanted to play outside, but they had chores to do.
"It won't take us long, Buz. Then we can go outside.
If we clean up fast, we will have time for a fast ride."

Budger was the first one to put toys away.
Buz stared out the window; he wanted to play.
"Come on, Buz, let's get this room clean, clean, clean."
That's when Budger saw something he had never seen.

It was round and plump and shaped like a bean.
It had two legs, two arms, and the color was green.
It seemed to be whispering into Buz's ear.
Budger moved closer so that he could hear.

I hope I don't have to clean and stay inside.
I hope I don't have to miss a good fast ride.
I hope I don't have to do it. I won't, won't, won't.
Those were the words coming from the green Hopeidont.

Budger got whispers from a strange-looking fellow.
It was small but plump, and its color was yellow.
"Don't listen to him, Buz, his words are all wrong.
Let's clean this mess quick; it won't take long."

"I hope I don't forget to do my part.
I hope I don't forget to finish what I start.
I hope I don't lose patience, and waste my time.
I hope I don't forget to clean up all this slime."

"Don't make me angry!" Budger heard from Buz.
Making people angry is what a green Hopeidont does.
"I want to go out and play, I don't want to be a cleaner."
And the more he got frustrated, his Hopeidont turned greener.

"You only have two hours according to my watch,
And then it's time to eat dinner," said Grandmasquatch.
"I'll help you get started, but then it's up to you.
You must be responsible for the things that you do."

"It won't take us long to complete this here chore.
Then we'll have so much fun just outside that door."
Although Buz was slower, Budger's patience grew.
And he led by example, like smart Bigfoots do.

Buz was feeling silly that he had made such a scene.
His Hopeidont changed color; it was no longer green.
"I hope you forgive me for the words that I said."
Buz was so embarrassed that his Hopeidont turned red.

Budger could see that Buz was starting to mellow.
And the more he relaxed, his Hopeidont turned yellow.
Buz was getting whispers, right into his ear,
Speaking words of patience, that all kids should hear.

"I hope I don't forget to help when I'm asked.
I hope I don't get angry and get GREEN so fast.
I hope I don't lose patience when I want to go out and play.
I hope I don't listen to what green Hopeidonts say."

They had two hours for fun when they went outside.
So they jumped on the squatchbikes and went for a ride.
Budger enjoyed playing with this friend when he was happy, kind,
patient and mellow. So he looks for Hopeidonts that are not green or red
but the color of YELLOW !

BEDTIME THANK YOU

There are many things I think in my brain.
How you give me love and then love me again.
How you love me with time and love me with joy.
You love me with kindness and sometimes a toy.
You are the very thing I love most in my day,
And I've been thinking of words I'd like to say,
Words from my heart and what I remember,
For loving me each day, January through December.
I hope I don't forget to say thank you
For the time that you give, and all that you do.
I hope I don't keep growing, cause I sure like to climb
Into your lap for a story at bedtime.
I hope I will remember this time we have now,
So when I grow up big, I will always know how
To love with my time and love with my heart
Each day to the end, each day from the start.

RELAXED

Buz was so relaxed that his body felt like Jell-O. And the more he relaxed, his Hopeidont turned

_ _ _ _ _ .

Robbie Robin saw Buz sleeping by the tree as she flew. She was sad her friend was sleeping and her Hopeidont turned

_ _ _ _ _ .

Buz got irritated and was acting cranky and mean, but he took a quick nap so his Hopeidont would not turn

_ _ _ _ _ .

Her Hopeidont was orange as Buz slept till noon, and Robbie Robin was hopeful he would wake

_ _ _ _ .

(Hint: **Not** a color)

Being embarrassed can make you feel small,

but choosing to be strong
will make you ten feet tall.

EMBARRASSED.

Buz was embarrassed that the wind was dead; his kite was now stuck and his Hopeidont turned

_ _ _.

Buz was irritated, cranky and started acting mean. Budger calmed him down so his Hopeidont would not turn

_ _ _ _.

Although Budger wished they could make the tree shrink, he was open to climbing, so his Hopeidont turned

_ _ _ _.

Buz was confused and unsure and didn't know what to say. He didn't know how to fix it, and his Hopeidont turned

_ _ _ _.

ANGRY

Buz was watching a new show that he had never seen, but his TV broke and now his Hopeidont turned

_ _ _ _ _ .

When the TV broke, Buz's disappointment grew, but his Hopeidont didn't turn green; this time it turned

_ _ _ _ .

When Grandmasquatch asked Buz how the TV broke, he didn't know what to say. And when Buz is unsure and confused, his Hopeidont turns

_ _ _ _ .

Buz was almost ready to explode and got right to the brink, but learning how to stay calm makes his Hopeidont turn

_ _ _ _ .

It's easy to enjoy something while you're all alone,

But nothing says happy like sharing a cone!

Budger could not be more happy when he got ice cream from a fellow. He smiled so big that his Hopeidont turned

_ _ _ _ _ _ .

Budger likes ice cream in a big round circle. It makes others so jealous that their Hopeidonts turn

_ _ _ _ _ _ .

Buz's Hopeidont was orange from all the anticipation. He was so excited, he gave Budger a standing

_ _ _ _ _ _ _ .

(Hint: **Not** a color)

Budger was regretful when he remembered all the friends he knew. There wasn't enough ice cream for all, and now his Hopeidont turned

_ _ _ _ .

Being shy is never easy, but friends will help you be strong, not uneasy.

SHY

Budger was shy, but the animals wanted to know what he had read. So Budger shared his book even though his Hopeidont turned

_ _ _ _.

Budger was unsure of what his new friends would say, and the more he was unsure, his Hopeidont turned

_ _ _ _ _.

Budger felt peaceful, calm, and mellow. And because his new friends were being kind, Budger's Hopeidont turned

_ _ _ _ _ _ _.

Budger was no longer worried about what the animals would think. He was so open to share his book that his Hopeidont turned

_ _ _ _ _.

FRUSTRATED

Buz got frustrated when he stepped in something unseen. Getting gum off his foot makes his Hopeidont turn

_ _ _ _ _ _.

Blowing a bubble makes Budger nice and mellow. He's so relaxed that his Hopeidont is turning

_ _ _ _ _ _.

When Buz stepped in this gum, it really ruined his day. He felt so awkward that his Hopeidont turned.

_ _ _ _.

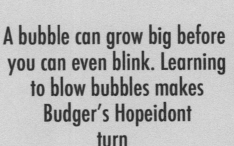

A bubble can grow big before you can even blink. Learning to blow bubbles makes Budger's Hopeidont turn

_ _ _ _.

The best part about friendship is sharing and caring.

Just make sure what you share is not dangerous and daring.

JOYFUL

When Buz received balloons,
he stopped to
bellow, "I'm so joyful,
my Hopeidont
just turned

_ _ _ _ _ _ ."

Buz was depressed that his friend,
Budger was not there too,
and the more he missed
his friend, his Hopeidont
turned

_ _ _ _ .

Buz's Hopeidont turns orange
when he's this high in the air.
He gets so excited that it's
giving him quite a

_ _ _ _ _ .

(Hint: **Not** a color)

Robbie Robin heard exactly
what Buz said,
"I'm afraid of heights"
and his Hopeidont
turned

_ _ _ .

If you are worried and scared, then turn to a friend.

You will be safer and glad when the worry comes to an end.

WORRIED

Randall Rabbit was worried about the thought in his head. "If this lightning gets closer, my Hopeidont will turn

_ _ _ . "

Bringing a rain coat is what Budger suggested Buz should do. Buz was regretful he didn't listen, and his Hopeidont turned

_ _ _ _.

Buz was open to the words that Randall said, so he stopped to think. And the more he thought about Randall's advice, his Hopeidont turned

_ _ _ _.

Buz's Hopeidont turned purple because he was suspicious and wary. He thought if he kept going the way he was, the storm would really be

_ _ _ _ _.

(Hint: **Not** a color)

Being respectful of others when what you do is loud

will make your family happy, patient, and proud.

IRRITATED

Buz was irritated that Budger was making such a scene. The louder Budger blew his horn, Buz's Hopeidont turned

_ _ _ _ _ .

Budger was never shy about blowing his horn no matter what Buz said. If Budger had been shy, his Hopeidont would have turned

_ _ _ .

Budger was insecure about blowing his horn and ruining Buz's day, but it was only for a minute that his Hopeidont turned

_ _ _ _ .

Buz's Hopeidont was turning purple, and he was really doubting that Budger would ever stop even when Buz started

_ _ _ _ _ _ _ .

(Hint: **Not** a color)

Have you ever been so nervous that you don't know what to do?

Don't feel bad, Buz feels nervous too!

NERVOUS

Buz was nervous
that he'd fall on his head.
He was so nervous that
his Hopeidont turned

_ _ _.

Buz is scared of falling and
his life is holding up by a thread.
This has him full of fear and
his Hopeidont is turning

_ _ _.

Buz's Hopeidont turns orange
when he gets very surprised.
You can see it in his arms,
mouth, and especially his

_ _ _ _.

(Hint: **Not** a color)

Buz was very receptive to
balancing on this ball,
but he didn't stop to think.
Now he's stuck on this ball
way up high and his
Hopeidont is turning

_ _ _ _.

OFFENDED

Buz feels offended because what the squirrel did was mean. He's so offended, his Hopeidont is starting to turn

_ _ _ _ _ .

Buz feels insecure and doesn't know what to say. It makes him so insecure, his Hopeidont is turning

_ _ _ _ .

That squirrel has Buz chasing him in a circle. He can't trust him anymore, so his Hopeidont is turning

_ _ _ _ _ _ .

If someone sees the mustache, Buz is worried about what will be said. When Buz gets worried and embarrassed, his Hopeidont turns

_ _ _ .

Taking time with your closest friend is what we all can do.

Have you reminded your friends what they mean to you?

PEACEFUL

The sunset was so peaceful that Buz and Budger started to mellow. And the more peaceful they got, their Hopeidont turned

_ _ _ _ _ _ .

Buz and Budger were hopeful that the sunset would never end. Their Hopeidonts turn

_ _ _ _ _ _

when they are hopeful with a friend.

Their day was really improving as the sun started to sink. The sunset made their day so much better, their Hopeidont turned

_ _ _ _ .

The two Bigfoots were so lucky to find such a view. It made them sad to leave, and now their Hopeidont turned

_ _ _ _ .

In the Home...

This book was given to _____

Who gave me this book? _____

My grade is _____

The color of my Hopeidont when I got this book was? _____

In School...

My teacher's name is _____

What color is my Hopeidont when I think about my teacher? _____

Which Hopeidont do I want to understand better with the help of my teacher? _____

Which color is my Hopeidont when I'm at school? _____

Which color is my Hopeidont when I learn something new? _____

In a Children's Hospital...

What is the name of my local Children's Hospital? _____

What is the website of my local Children's Hospital? _____

What is the color of my Hopeidont when I think about kids at Children's Hospital? _____

What is the color of my Hopeidont when I think about helping others? _____

What is the color of my Hopeidont when I see a kid get better? _____

I have two daughters that mean the world to me, so on every spread in the picture story there is an E and a G.
"E" for Ellie and "G" for Gracie, if you'd like to know, so be patient, look hard, take your time, and go very, very slow.

- Franklin Smith

HOPEiDONT BOOKS

Creating resources for every family, child, and teacher

Books that build character and relationship skills.
Collect the whole series! Books available EXCLUSIVELY at HOPEIDONT.COM

You buy a book and Hopeidont Books donates a book
When you purchase a book from Hopeidont Books on the website, we will donate a book to a child fighting for their health and wellness, or a teacher that is fighting to make our children ready for the world.

Why children's hospitals?
Learning to be a high character person is hard enough for a child, but when you add in the struggle for life, health, and wellness, that challenge becomes even greater. Teaching a child to give to someone who is in need and fighting courageously is good for the sick child and family, but it also introduces your child to considering the needs of others. This builds character and ultimately creates a path to managing strong relationships. Your child can visit our website and write a note of encouragement to accompany the books being donated to children's hospitals . This becomes another teachable moment for the parent or guardian, and it gives the child a chance to express their thoughts and feelings.

Why teachers?
It is easy to love teachers who spend so much time caring for our children and teaching kids how to be creative in their search for knowledge. However, that search for knowledge can be expensive for teachers. Many people do not realize that teachers buy most of the storybooks that are read in class out of their own pocket. If you choose to donate a book to a teacher, Hopeidont Books will send an extra copy to you so that your child can encourage the teacher with a gift. Apples are great, but a book makes an impact on the whole class. Doesn't it make sense to give something special to the ones who make such an investment in your child?

Express yourself through words and pictures here!

Express yourself through words and pictures!

Download the coloring pages
on the Hopeidont Books website for free!

www.hopeidont.com

The more interactive children are with building their character
and managing their emotions, the more effective they will be in their relationships.

Order books exclusively at
www.hopeidont.com